5-G Challenge
Doing Life with God in the Picture

Administrator's Guidebook

WILLOW CREEK RESOURCES®

Lesson-by-lesson instructions
for administrating the curriculum and
reproducible pages for Small Group activities

Administrator's Guidebook
5-G Challenge: Doing Life with God in the Picture
Spring Quarter Grades 2/3

Copyright© 2001 Willow Creek Community Church
ISBN 0-744-125-529

Requests for information should be addressed to:
Willow Creek Association
P.O. Box 3188
Barrington, IL 60011-3188

Executive Director of Promiseland: Sue Miller

Executive Director of Promiseland Publishing: Nancy Raney

Editorial Team: Jorie Dahlin, Janet Quinn, Nancy Raney

Designer: Kathee Biaggne
Cover and Interior Illustrator: Laurie Keller

Many thanks to: the Promiseland staff team as a whole who continually contributes, our volunteers who help put supplies together each weekend, and the volunteers who try out, test, and evaluate this curriculum to give us feedback along the way.

WILLOW CREEK RESOURCES®

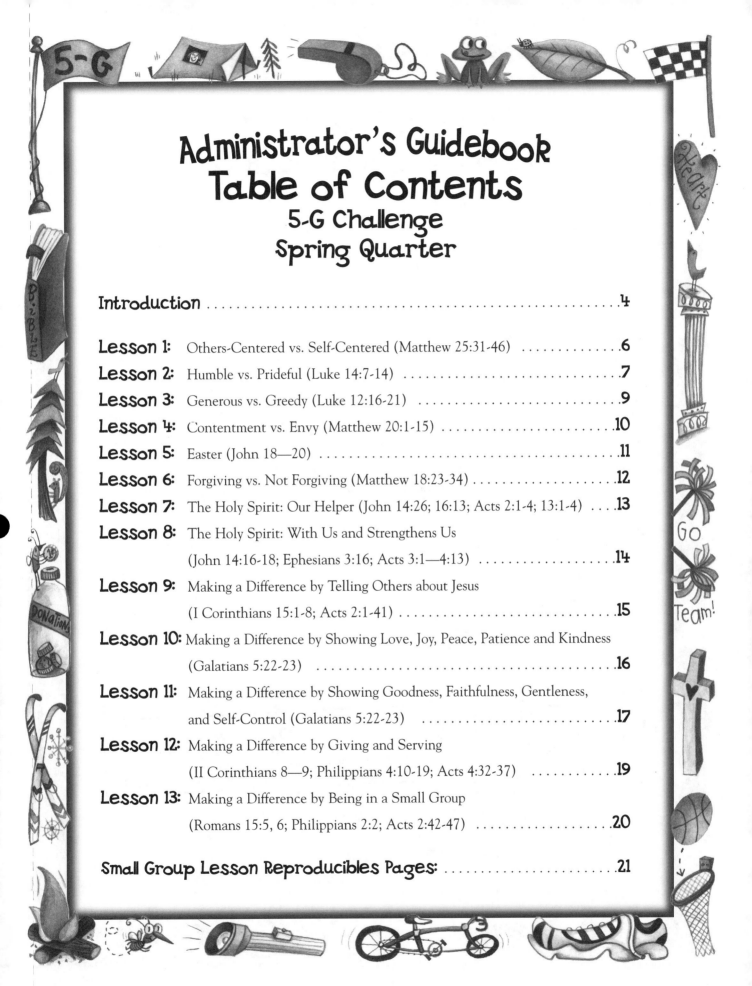

Administrator's Guidebook
Table of Contents
5-G Challenge
Spring Quarter

Introduction
to Administrator's Guidebook

The administration of a children's ministry program is a role filled with details. The role of the Administrator is vital to the success of the Promiseland Curriculum. This *Administrator's Guidebook* is designed to help you, the Administrator, see at a glance the tasks that need to be accomplished for each lesson. Within the Promiseland Curriculum lessons are three components: Activity Stations, Large Group Program, and Small Group Time. Each of these components will have a leader giving oversight to what occurs there.

It is recommended that the leader of the Activity Stations be someone who has the spiritual gift of administration. Therefore, that person may or may not need the assistance of you, the Administrator of the entire *5-G Challenge* Promiseland Curriculum.

The leaders of the Large Group Program and Small Groups may or may not have administration as one of their primary spiritual gifts. Their spiritual gifts may be creative communication, teaching, and shepherding. Because of this, they may need your assistance in administrating the details of their presentations. This assistance may involve gathering props, cueing up videos, making photocopies, or securing equipment. The *Large Group* and *Small Group Guidebooks* give detailed instructions for any construction or assembly needs.

Included in this *Administrator's Guidebook* are all of the reproducible pages for the Small Group Leaders. There is an identifier at the bottom of each reproducible page that indicates the lesson which uses that page.

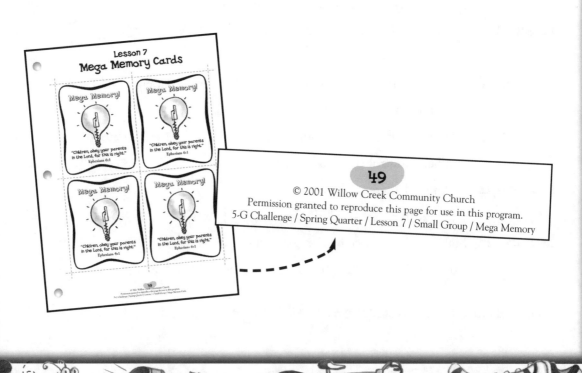

Involving Others

This guidebook lists all of the details that need to be addressed for each lesson. It is not the Administrator's responsibility to DO all the tasks, but rather, to assist and coordinate others so the details are taken care of. Even though the Large Group Teacher may not have the gift of administration, he or she will most likely desire to give input in the creation of the teaching props and environment.

Use this guidebook as a tool to make assignments to other leaders and volunteers so the details are addressed. Volunteers who are unable to commit to being present during the actual ministry time may be able to volunteer a couple of hours a week to assist in preparing for the week's lesson. Create a daytime team who can volunteer on a regular basis to put together the materials for the Small Group Leaders' bins. This is a wonderful way to build community with

volunteers! Also, this is a great place for seeker parents to be involved and assist in some behind-the-scenes needs.

Lesson 1

Unit 1: Cross Training
Others-Centered vs. Self-Centered

Activity Stations:
- Choose activities that will work best for this lesson.
- Assist with setup.
- Confirm any guests you have scheduled.
- Offer your support in any way needed.

Large Group Supplies:
- ○ STOP sign
- ○ Self-centered sign
- ○ Bible Verse sign
- ○ Music for transitions and singing
- ○ Filled lunch bag
- ○ Football
- ○ Skateboard
- ○ 2 Flip charts/markers
- ○ *Optional: Doing Life with God in the Picture CD*

Equipment Needs:
- ○ CD player

In Advance *(Work with the Large Group Producer to administrate the following):*
- Determine which songs you will use and be prepared to lead or teach them.
- Recruit an instrumental musician. This musician will play a short piece on the instrument to illustrate training versus trying.
- Gather props and set teaching area. Put the lunch bag, football, and skateboard off to the side where you can retrieve them easily. If you don't have a skateboard, you can substitute rollerblades, a scooter, or a bike. Set flip charts and STOP sign off to the side where you can get them easily during the lesson.
- Create STOP sign. Cut red posterboard into an octagon (eight sides). Use white paint, white tape, or strips of white paper to write STOP on the sign. Store it carefully, as you will use it for the next few weeks. Create Self-centered sign by writing "Self-Centered vs. Others-Centered" on a piece of posterboard.
- Prepare Bible Verse sign.

Small Group Supplies:
- ○ Bases
- ○ Score Cards
- ○ Game Cards
- ○ Game Pieces
- ○ Pencil

In Advance:
- Photocopy and cut out Bible Verse Cards—one per child (page 27).
- Photocopy and cut out Bases—one set per group (page 21).
- Photocopy and cut out Score Cards—one per group (page 26).
- Photocopy and cut out Game Cards—one set per group (pages 22-25).
- Gather Game Pieces—one per child. These can be erasers, candies, small toys, or small numbered squares of paper.
- Gather pencils—one per group.

Lesson 2

Unit 1: Cross Training
Humble vs. Prideful

Activity Stations:
- Choose activities that will work best for this lesson.
- Assist with setup.
- Confirm any guests you have scheduled.
- Offer your support in any way needed.

Large Group Supplies:
- ○ STOP sign
- ○ Pride sign
- ○ Humble sign
- ○ Sports video clip
- ○ Bible Verse sign
- ○ Music for transitions and singing
- ○ 5-G Challenge Video— Spring Quarter
- ○ Optional: Doing Life with God in the Picture CD

Equipment Needs:
- ○ CD player
- ○ TV/VCR

In Advance (Work with the Large Group Producer to administrate the following):
- Determine which songs you will use and be prepared to lead or teach them.

- Choose a sports video clip. Buy, borrow, or check out a video from the library that shows an Olympic or professional athlete doing something great, such as scoring a touchdown in football, shooting a slam-dunk in basketball, or scoring a perfect "ten" in gymnastics. You could possibly record a sports clip off of TV. The Small Group game is based on football, so you may want to find a football clip. (If you use a professional video, check it to see if you need permission to show it in a public setting. Call the Motion Picture Licensing Corporation for more information at 800-515-8855.)
- Gather props and set teaching area. Gather STOP sign from last week's lesson, and put it on your teaching area.
- Make Pride sign by writing, "Pride: Thinking you are better than everyone else" on a piece of posterboard.

Make Humble sign by writing, "Humble: Putting others first" on a piece of posterboard.
- Prepare Bible Verse sign.
- Cue up 5-G Challenge Video to Lesson 2.

Small Group Supplies:
- ○ Football Field
- ○ Paper Football
- ○ Game Cards
- ○ Score Card
- ○ Die
- ○ Pencil

In Advance:
- Photocopy and cut out Bible Verse Cards—one per child (page 33).
- Punch out the Football Field pages. Cut the inside edge off of one of the pages, and tape the pages together so they line up to create one whole Football Field. Photocopy this Football Field onto 11-by-17-inch paper—one per group (pages 30-31).
- Photocopy and cut out Score Cards—one per group (page 32).

(cont. on p. 8)

Lesson 2 (cont.)

- Photocopy and cut out Game Cards—one set per group (pages 28-29).
- Prepare paper football— one per group. For each football, cut an 8 1/2-by-2 1/2-inch strip of paper.

Fold the strip in half lengthwise. Starting at a short end, fold a bottom edge flush against the long edge, forming a triangle. Continue folding as you would fold a flag until you

are left with one thick triangle. Tape the triangle together.
- Gather pencils and dice— one of each per group.

Lesson 3

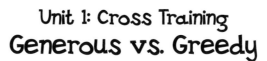

Unit 1: Cross Training
Generous vs. Greedy

Activity Stations:
- Choose activities that will work best for this lesson.
- Assist with setup.
- Confirm any guests you have scheduled.
- Offer your support in any way needed.

Large Group Supplies:
- ○ STOP sign
- ○ Generous sign
- ○ Greedy sign
- ○ 10-15 balloons
- ○ Black permanent marker
- ○ Bible
- ○ Bible Verse sign
- ○ Music for transitions and singing
- ○ "Scuba" gear
- ○ XXL adult shirt
- ○ *Optional: Making It Connect CD*
- ○ *Optional: Doing Life with God in the Picture CD*

Equipment Needs:
- ○ CD player

In Advance *(Work with the Large Group Producer to administrate the following):*
- Determine which songs you will use and be prepared to lead or teach them.
- Recruit people needed.

- Photocopy script (pages 30-33 in *Large Group Programming Guidebook*) and rehearse teaching time.
- Gather materials to make pretend scuba gear. You will need flippers, goggles, extension cord, and a canister vacuum or leaf blower. Secure the vacuum or leaf blower to your back to look like a scuba tank. (The lesson refers to a vacuum, but you can use a leaf blower just as easily.)
- Get an XXL long-sleeved shirt for a child to wear during the balloon activity.
- Blow up balloons. Write one thing kids want on each balloon with the permanent marker. Write specific names of candy, games, video games, electronic equipment, and toys.
- Prepare Bible Verse sign.
- Create Generous sign by writing, "Generous: giving freely to others" on a piece of posterboard. Create Greedy sign by writing, "Greedy: keeping everything for yourself" on a piece of posterboard.
- Gather props and set teaching area. Gather STOP sign from last

week's lesson, and put it on your teaching area. Put balloons and shirt in a large container or garbage can on your teaching area.
- Prepare a 1-minute story about a time someone was generous to you.

Small Group Supplies
- ○ Hockey Rinks
- ○ Game Cards
- ○ Score Cards/Pencils
- ○ Pennies

In Advance:
- Photocopy and cut out Bible Verse Cards—one per child (page 37).
- Photocopy and cut out Game Cards—one set per every two children (pages 34-35).
- Photocopy and cut out Score Cards—one per every two children (page 36).
- Gather posterboard—one piece per every two children. Using a thick, black marker, draw a hockey goal at both ends of the posterboard. Draw a line down the middle of the posterboard. This will be the hockey rink.
- Gather pennies—three for every two children.
- Gather pencils—one per every two children.

Lesson 4

Unit 1: Cross Training
Contentment vs. Envy

Activity Stations:
- Choose activities that will work best for this lesson.
- Assist with setup.
- Confirm any guests you have scheduled.
- Offer your support in any way needed.

Large Group Supplies:
- ☐ Contentment sign
- ☐ Envy sign
- ☐ STOP sign
- ☐ 2 bags of candy
- ☐ Bible Verse sign
- ☐ Large bin or trash can filled with toys, clothes
- ☐ Saltine crackers
- ☐ Cupcakes
- ☐ Old t-shirt
- ☐ New brand-name sweatshirt
- ☐ Old soccer ball
- ☐ New soccer ball
- ☐ Music for transitions and singing
- ☐ Bible
- ☐ *Optional: Doing Life with God in the Picture CD*

Equipment Needs:
- ☐ CD player

In Advance *(Work with the Large Group Producer to administrate the following):*
- Determine which songs you will use and be prepared to lead or teach them.
- Recruit Assistant.
- Rehearse teaching time.
- Prepare Bible Verse sign.
- Create Contentment sign by writing, "Contentment: being happy with what you have" on a piece of posterboard. Create Envy sign by writing, "Envy: Wanting other peoples' stuff" on a piece of posterboard.
- Gather props and set teaching area. Gather STOP sign from last week's lesson, and put it on your teaching area. Fill a large bin or trash can with any toys, clothes, and other items. Dump out the trash can onto your teaching area.
- Gather Content versus Envy example items and put them in a box or bin: saltine crackers, cupcakes, old t-shirt, new sweatshirt, old soccer ball, new soccer ball. You can substitute other items if you'd like, but be sure to choose a simple item and a nicer or more elaborate item for each example.

Small Group Supplies:
- ☐ Buckets marked with S, T, O, and P
- ☐ Bean bags
- ☐ Score Card
- ☐ Game Cards

- ☐ Pencil
- ☐ Tape

In Advance:
- Photocopy and cut out Bible Verse Cards—one per child (page 42).
- Photocopy and cut out Score Cards—one per group (page 41).
- Photocopy and cut out Game Cards—one set per group (pages 38-40).
- Gather buckets—a set of four buckets per group. These can be cardboard or plastic buckets from fast food restaurants or discount stores. Check your art supply cabinet for buckets, or see if your church maintenance staff has any you could use. Write one letter on each bucket: S, T, O, and P. If you can't write directly on the buckets, write the letters on paper, then tape the paper to the buckets.
- Gather bean bags—two per group. You can use another small object instead, such as Ping Pong balls, erasers, or marbles.
- Gather masking tape—one roll per group. Groups can share rolls if necessary.
- Gather pencils—one per group.

Lesson 5

Unit 1: Cross Training
Easter

Activity Stations:
- Choose activities that will work best for this lesson.
- Assist with setup.
- Confirm any guests you have scheduled.
- Offer your support in any way needed.

Large Group Supplies:
- ○ Bible Verse sign
- ○ "Angry mob" sound effect
- ○ Rope
- ○ Toy sword
- ○ Celebration music
- ○ Disciple costume (Bible times robe)
- ○ Pilate costume (royal robes)
- ○ Mary costume (Bible times robe/head covering)
- ○ Music for transitions and singing
- ○ 5 Stations materials
- ○ 5 No Way signs
- ○ *Optional: Doing Life with God in the Picture CD*

Equipment Needs:
- ○ CD player

In Advance *(Work with the Large Group Producer to administrate the following)*:
- Determine which songs you will sing and be prepared to lead or teach them.
- Gather supplies and set teaching area.
- Photocopy script (pages 43-45 in *Large Group Programming Guidebook*) and rehearse teaching time with Assistant and CD Player Assistant.
- Prepare Bible Verse sign.
- Prepare five No Way signs. Write "NO WAY" in thick black marker on five pieces of cardstock. Depending on how your stations are made, plan to hang, tape, or pin them to the stations.
- Choose celebration music. Use any upbeat, happy-sounding music. For example, you might use Steven Curtis Chapman's "Prologue" off of his *Great Adventure* CD.
- Gather costumes.

- Gather or prepare an "Angry mob" sound effect. You can create one with a group of people if you'd like.
- Gather equipment and prepare the 5 stations. You can make the stations as detailed or as simple as you'd like. Suggestions are in the *Large Group Programming Guidebook*.
- Set up stations around your teaching area. See diagram in Large Group Programming Guidebook.

Small Group Supplies:
- ○ Easter Story Pictures (sets of 11)

In Advance:
- Photocopy and cut out Bible Verse Cards—one per child (page 45).
- Photocopy and cut out Easter Story Pictures—one set of eleven per every two children (pages 43-44).
- Place the above-mentioned items in a bin for each Small Group Leader.

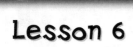

Lesson 6

Unit 1: Cross Training
Forgiving vs. Not forgiving

Activity Stations:
- Choose activities that will work best for this lesson.
- Assist with setup.
- Confirm any guests you have scheduled.
- Offer your support in any way needed.

Large Group Supplies:
- ⭘ Forgive sign
- ⭘ Don't Forgive sign
- ⭘ STOP sign
- ⭘ Bible Verse sign
- ⭘ Friend sign
- ⭘ "Gimme Jimmy" sign
- ⭘ "Big Al" sign
- ⭘ Crown
- ⭘ Blender
- ⭘ Muffin pan
- ⭘ "Doughnut" ingredients
- ⭘ Matches
- ⭘ Chair or stool
- ⭘ Music for transitions and singing
- ⭘ Bible
- ⭘ *Optional: Doing Life with God in the Picture CD*

Equipment Needs:
- ⭘ CD player

In Advance *(Work with the Large Group Producer to administrate the following)*:

- Determine which songs you will use and be prepared to lead or teach them.
- Rehearse teaching time.
- Prepare Bible Verse sign.
- Create Forgiving sign by writing, "Forgive: Choosing to stop being mad at some one; pardoning or excusing someone" on a piece of posterboard. Create Not Forgiving sign by writing, "Don't Forgive: Holding a grudge; staying angry" on a piece of posterboard. Create "Friend" sign, "Gimme Jimmy" sign, and "Big Al" sign by writing those phrases on 8 1/2-by-11-inch cardstock or cardboard. Affix string to them so volunteers can hang them around their necks.
- Gather props and set teaching area. See instructions in *Large Group Programming Guidebook.*
- Gather supplies to make "doughnuts." You can use any silly ingredients you have on hand. The lesson refers to canned pineapple, chocolate cupcake, kidney beans, and root beer.

Small Group Supplies:
- ⭘ S, T, O, P Cards (2 sets)
- ⭘ Plain paper

- ⭘ Ping-Pong balls
- ⭘ Medals
- ⭘ Ribbon/String

In Advance:
- Photocopy and cut out Bible Verse Cards—one per child (page 48).
- Photocopy and cut out STOP Cards—two sets per group (page 47).
- Photocopy and cut out Stop Medals onto brightly colored cardstock—one per child (page 46). Punch a hole in the top of the medals. If you don't have time to cut out medals, put children's scissors in the Small Group Leaders' bins, and let them know kids will cut out their own medals.
- Gather paper—18 sheets or more per group. This can be any 8 1/2-by-11-inch paper. (It can be scratch paper, because the kids will make paper airplanes out of it, and crumple it to toss in a basket.)
- Gather Ping-Pong balls—two per group.
- Gather ribbon or string—cut a 2-foot piece for every child.
- Place the above-mentioned items into a bin for each Small Group Leader.

Lesson 7

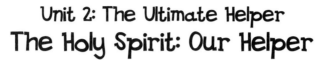

Unit 2: The Ultimate Helper
The Holy Spirit: Our Helper

Activity Stations:
- Choose activities that will work best for this lesson.
- Assist with setup.
- Confirm any guests you have scheduled.
- Offer your support in any way needed.

Large Group Supplies:
- ❍ Bible Verse sign
- ❍ Music for transitions and singing
- ❍ World sign
- ❍ Cross sign
- ❍ Child sign
- ❍ Father, Son, and Holy Spirit Signs
- ❍ 15 colored paper squares
- ❍ Marker
- ❍ Thumb tacks
- ❍ 3 drinking cups
- ❍ Hide it in Your Heart Cards
- ❍ Bulletin board(s)
- ❍ *Optional: Doing Life with God in the Picture CD*

Equipment Needs:
- ❍ CD player

In Advance *(Work with the Large Group Producer to administrate the following)*:
- Determine which songs you will use and be prepared to lead or teach them.
- Rehearse teaching time.
- Enlarge the World, Cross, and Child signs (on page 60 of the *Large Group Programming Guidebook*) to the size of a piece of posterboard, about 27 x 32 inches. If you have a big classroom, be sure all signs are large enough to be seen from the back of the room. You can take signs to a copy shop to have them enlarged. Or, photocopy the signs onto a transparency sheet. Put the transparency sheet on an overhead projector so the sign is projected onto a piece of posterboard hanging on the wall. Trace the object onto the posterboard.
- Photocopy the Hide it in Your Heart Cards onto colored paper (page 59 of the *Large Group Programming Guidebook*). Crumple them up and put them on your teaching area with the three drinking cups.
- Prepare Father, Son, and Holy Spirit signs on 8 1/2 x 11 in. cardstock. Write "Father" on a brightly-colored piece of cardstock. Write "Son" on a brightly-colored piece of cardstock. Write "Holy Spirit" on a brightly-colored piece of cardstock.
- Gather props and set teaching area. Post World, Cross, and Child signs on a large rolling bulletin board on your teaching area. If you don't have a large bulletin board, use three smaller boards.
- Prepare Bible Verse sign.

Small Group Supplies:
- ❍ Paper
- ❍ Pencils
- ❍ Mega Memory Cards

In Advance:
- Photocopy and cut out Bible Verse Cards—one per child (page 50).
- Photocopy and cut out Mega Memory Cards—one set per group (page 49).
- Gather paper—four sheets per group.
- Gather pencils—four per group.
- Place the above-mentioned items in a bin for each Small Group Leader.

13

Lesson 8

Unit 2: The Ultimate Helper
The Holy Spirit: With Us and Strengthens Us

Activity Stations:
- Choose activities that will work best for this lesson.
- Assist with setup.
- Confirm any guests you have scheduled.
- Offer your support in any way needed.

Large Group Supplies:
- ◯ Remember, Ask, and Do signs
- ◯ Child sign (from Lesson 7)
- ◯ 3 lamps with extension cords
- ◯ Money
- ◯ 2 Backpacks/school bags
- ◯ Chair
- ◯ Watch
- ◯ TV remote control
- ◯ School book
- ◯ Pencil
- ◯ Bible Verse sign
- ◯ Music for transitions and singing
- ◯ *Doing Life with God in the Picture* CD

Equipment Needs:
- ◯ CD player

In Advance *(Work with the Large Group Producer to administrate the following)*:
- Determine which songs you will sing and be prepared to lead or teach them.
- Recruit people needed.
- Photocopy the script (pages 63-67 in *Large Group Programming Guidebook*) for the three Jr. High or High School students and rehearse the teaching time.
- Retrieve the Child sign from Lesson 7 and place it on your teaching area.
- Prepare Bible Verse sign.
- Prepare to play the song "STOP," from the *Doing Life with God in the Picture* CD during the third monologue.
- Prepare Remember, Ask, and Do signs by writing each word in thick black marker on a strip of brightly-colored paper. Be sure the writing is large enough so kids sitting in the back can see it. Put tape on the backs of the signs, so you can stick them to the lamps during the lesson.
- Gather props and set teaching area. See instructions in the *Large Group Programming Guidebook*.

Small Group Supplies:
- ◯ Craft noodles
- ◯ Sponge
- ◯ Power Cards
- ◯ Erasers
- ◯ Cardstock

In Advance:
- Photocopy and cut out Bible Verse Cards—one per child (page 53).
- Photocopy and cut out Power Cards—one set per group (pages 51-52).
- Gather craft noodles—32 per group. Craft noodles look like packing peanuts, and they stick together when you wet them. You can use biodegradable packing peanuts as well. You can find craft noodles at craft stores or in craft catalogs.
- Gather sponges—one per group.
- Gather novelty erasers—three per group. These are small erasers shaped like animals or people, found in party stores, or in craft catalogs. If you do not have erasers, you can use other small objects, such as pennies or paper clips.
- Gather cardstock—two sheets per group (any color).
- Place the above-mentioned items in a bin for each Small Group Leader.

Lesson 9

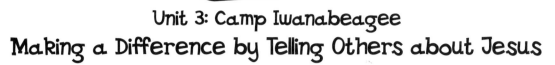

Unit 3: Camp Iwanabeagee
Making a Difference by Telling Others about Jesus

Activity Stations:
- Choose activities that will work best for this lesson.
- Assist with setup.
- Confirm any guests you have scheduled.
- Offer your support in any way needed.

Large Group Supplies:
- ❍ Grace Flag
- ❍ ABC sign
- ❍ Bible Verse sign
- ❍ Flip chart/marker
- ❍ Campfire (rocks and logs)
- ❍ *Camp Iwanabeagee* CD
- ❍ Music for transitions and singing
- ❍ *Optional: Doing Life with God in the Picture CD*

Costumes:
- ❍ Camp Counselor clothes

Equipment Needs:
- ❍ CD player

In Advance (*Work with the Large Group Producer to administrate the following*):
- Determine which songs you will use and be prepared to lead or teach them.
- Have the teacher wear camp counselor gear, such as a hat, khaki shorts, hiking boots, and a t-shirt. You might carry a canteen, wear a whistle, etc.
- Recruit a CD Player Assistant.
- Photocopy the script (pages 74-78 in *Large Group Programming Guidebook*) and rehearse the teaching time.
- Listen to the *Camp Iwanabeagee* CD Tracks 4 and 6 so you know the Marching Chant and the Grace G Cheer.
- Prepare the Grace Flag by writing or painting GRACE on a bandana-sized square of brightly-colored fabric. You will need to post your flag in your teaching area. You can string it onto a flagpole, hang it from the ceiling, or post it on a bulletin board.
- Prepare Bible Verse sign.
- Prepare ABC sign by writing ABC on a piece of poster-board. Or, use an ABC sign or prop you have used in a previous salvation lesson.
- Gather props and set teaching area. See instructions in the *Large Group Programming Guidebook*.

Small Group Supplies:
- ❍ Invitations
- ❍ Markers
- ❍ Code Instruction Card
- ❍ Paper
- ❍ Envelopes

In Advance:
- Photocopy and cut out Bible Verse Cards—one per child (page 56).
- Fill your church information and service times into the Invitations. Then, photocopy Invitations—one per child (page 54). Cut off the page footer on the cutting line provided.
- Photocopy Code Instruction Cards—one per group (page 55).
- Gather paper—one sheet per child.
- Gather business-sized envelopes—one per child.
- Gather fine-tip markers or colored pencils—several per Small Group.
- Place the above-mentioned items in a bin for each Small Group Leader.

15

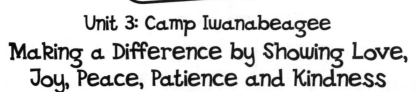

Lesson 10

Unit 3: Camp Iwanabeagee
Making a Difference by Showing Love, Joy, Peace, Patience and Kindness

Activity Stations:
- Choose activities that will work best for this lesson.
- Assist with setup.
- Confirm any guests you have scheduled.
- Offer your support in any way needed.

Large Group Supplies:
- ○ Growth Flag
- ○ Campfire (rocks and logs)
- ○ *Camp Iwanabeagee* CD
- ○ Bible Verse sign
- ○ Music for transitions and singing
- ○ *5-G Challenge* video—spring quarter
- ○ Fruit of the Spirit signs
- ○ Bulletin Board
- ○ Thumbtacks
- ○ Backpack
- ○ *Optional: Doing Life with God in the Picture CD*

Costumes:
- ○ Camp Counselor clothes

Equipment Needs:
- ○ CD player
- ○ TV/VCR

In Advance (*Work with the Large Group Producer to administrate the following*):

- Determine which songs you will use and be prepared to lead or teach them.
- Prepare the Growth Flag by writing or painting GROWTH on a bandana-sized square of brightly-colored fabric. You will need to post your flag in your teaching area. You can string it onto a flagpole, hang it from the ceiling, or post it on a bulletin board.
- Listen to the *Camp Iwanabeagee* CD Tracks 4 and 7 so you know the Marching Chant and the Growth G Cheer.
- Have the teacher wear camp counselor gear, such as a hat, khaki shorts, hiking boots, and a t-shirt. You might carry a canteen, whistle, or other camp gear.
- Recruit a CD Player Assistant.
- Prepare Bible Verse sign.
- Cue up video to Lesson 10— "Camp Iwanabeagee."
- Enlarge the Fruit of the Spirit signs (page 88 of the *Large Group Programming Guidebook*) onto brightly colored paper. Put the signs in a backpack.

- Gather props and set teaching area. See instructions in the *Large Group Programming Guidebook.*

Small Group Supplies:
- ○ Fruit Cards
- ○ Know Your Fruit Squares

In Advance:
- Photocopy and cut out Bible Verse Cards—one per child (page 60).
- Write a Parent Letter on your church's letterhead about the giving project taking place in two weeks—one per child (example on page 61).
- Photocopy Fruit Cards and cut apart—one set per group (pages 57-58).
- Photocopy Know Your Fruit Squares—one per child (page 59). If your Small Groups have chairs available for their use, you do not need these Squares.
- Place the above-mentioned items in a bin for each Small Group Leader.

16

Lesson 11

Unit 3: Camp Iwanabeagee
Making a Difference by Showing Goodness, Faithfulness, Gentleness, and Self-Control

Activity Stations:
- Choose activities that will work best for this lesson.
- Assist with setup.
- Confirm any guests you have scheduled.
- Offer your support in any way needed.

Large Group Supplies:
- ○ Growth Flag (used in Lesson 10)
- ○ Campfire (rocks and logs)
- ○ *Camp Iwanabeagee* CD
- ○ Bible Verse sign
- ○ Music for transitions and singing
- ○ Fruit of the Spirit signs (used in Lesson 10)
- ○ Fruit of the Spirit signs (new this week)
- ○ Bulletin Board
- ○ Thumbtacks
- ○ Backpack
- ○ Bag/Backpack
- ○ Rock
- ○ Crumpled map
- ○ Drama set: trees and stump/log/bucket

Costumes:
- ○ Camp Counselor clothes

Equipment Needs:
- ○ CD player

In Advance (*Work with the Large Group Producer to administrate the following*):
- Determine which songs you will use and be prepared to lead or teach them.
- Gather Growth Flag, used last week. You will need to post your flag in your teaching area. You can string it onto a flagpole, hang it from the ceiling, or post it on a bulletin board.
- Listen to the *Camp Iwanabeagee* CD tracks 4 and 7 so you know the Marching Chant and the Growth G Cheer.
- Have the teacher wear camp counselor gear, such as a hat, khaki shorts, hiking boots, and a t-shirt. You might carry a canteen, whistle, or other camp gear.
- Recruit a CD Player Assistant.
- Recruit two Jr. High or High School boys for the drama sketch.
- Photocopy the script (pages 93-94 in *Large Group Programming Guidebook*) and rehearse the drama.
- Prepare Bible Verse sign.
- Enlarge the Fruit of the

Spirit signs (page 96 of the *Large Group Programming Guidebook*) onto brightly colored paper. Put these signs in a backpack.
- Gather props and set teaching area. Create a campfire by piling a few logs on your area. Encircle the logs with rocks. If possible, put an orange light inside the logs, and turn it on at campfire time. Orange hazard lights (one blinking, one non-blinking) work great, as do orange Christmas tree lights. You may want to create a camp-like setting on your teaching area, painting a backdrop of a camp cabin, and setting fake Christmas trees, plants, and trees around the teaching area. This is a five-week unit, so store your props carefully so you can use them for all five weeks of programming.
- Set the bulletin board on your teaching area so you can attach the Fruit of the Spirit signs to it. Post last

(cont. on p. 18)

Lesson 11 (cont.)

week's Fruit of the Spirit signs on the bulletin board. Set the backpack with Fruit of the Spirit signs on the teaching area.

- Set up a spot on your teaching area for the drama. Create an alcove of trees by setting up a few fake Christmas trees, and fake or real plants. Place a stump, log, or large overturned bucket in the alcove of trees. Put nature items in the bag, as if the boys are collecting them for a scavenger hunt. Nick should have a piece of paper in his pocket. Put the crumpled map and rock in the bag. (You can photocopy part of a map, then crumple it up.)

Small Group Supplies:

Self Control Station: Bucket Relay

- ❍ 2 1-gallon buckets with 6 holes punched in the bottom
- ❍ 2 large aluminum roasting pans
- ❍ 2 1-gallon buckets filled with water
- ❍ 6 cups
- ❍ Tarp material to place on the floor to protect the carpet
- ❍ Instruction Sheet (page 62)

Goodness Station: Art

- ❍ Large pieces of butcher paper (1 piece for each Small Group)
- ❍ Markers
- ❍ Instruction Sheet (page 63)

Gentleness Station: Story

- ❍ Various pictures (clip art pictures of person, bike, hurt knee, playground equipment, school, super hero)
- ❍ Pencils
- ❍ Paper
- ❍ Instruction Sheet (page 64)

Faithfulness Station:

Body Spelling

- ❍ Paper
- ❍ Pencil
- ❍ Instruction Sheet (page 65)

In Advance:

- Photocopy and cut out Bible Verse Cards—one per child (page 66).
- Write a Parent Letter on your church's letterhead—one per child (example on page 67). This is similar to the letter about the giving project you passed out last week.
- Place the above-mentioned items in a bin for each Small Group Leader.
- Gather the Small Group Supplies listed above for the Stations. There are four stations, so if you have more than four Small Groups, two or more Small Groups will be at one station at one time. If this is true for your church, be sure to provide enough materials at each station.
- Set up the Stations around the classroom, but cover them with sheets so kids are not tempted to play with them during Large Group Time. Small Groups will rotate clockwise from station to station throughout Small Group time.
- Recruit someone to assign Small Groups to their initial stations, keep track of time, and ring a bell/shout every five minutes when it is time for Small Groups to switch stations. (Today's Teacher may be willing to do this.)

Lesson 12

Unit 3: Camp Iwanabeagee
Making a Difference by Giving and Serving

Activity Stations:
- Choose activities that will work best for this lesson.
- Assist with setup.
- Confirm any guests you have scheduled.
- Offer your support in any way needed.

Large Group Supplies:
- ○ Good Stewardship Flag
- ○ Gifts Flag
- ○ Time sign
- ○ Abilities sign
- ○ Resources sign
- ○ Campfire (rocks and logs)
- ○ *Camp Iwanabeagee* CD
- ○ Bible Verse sign
- ○ Music for transitions and singing
- ○ *Optional: Doing Life with God in the Picture CD*

Costumes:
- ○ Camp Counselor clothes

Equipment Needs:
- ○ CD player

In Advance *(Work with the Large Group Producer to administrate the following):*
- Determine which songs you will use and be prepared to lead or teach them.
- Prepare the Good Stewardship Flag and Gifts Flag by writing or painting GOOD STEWARDSHIP and GIFTS on bandana-sized squares of brightly-colored fabric. You will need to post your flag in your teaching area. You can string it onto a flagpole, hang it from the ceiling, or post it on a bulletin board.
- Listen to the *Camp Iwanabeagee* CD tracks 4, 8, and 9 so you know the Marching Chant and the Good Stewardship and Gifts G Cheers.
- Have the teacher wear camp counselor gear, such as a hat, khaki shorts, hiking boots, and a t-shirt. You might carry a canteen, whistle, or other camp gear.
- Recruit a CD Player Assistant.
- Prepare Bible Verse sign.
- Prepare the Time, Abilities, and Resources signs. Write "TIME" in thick marker on a piece of posterboard. On another piece, write "ABILITIES." On a third, write "RESOURCES."

- Gather props and set teaching area. See set ideas in the *Large Group Programming Guidebook.*

Small Group Supplies:
- ○ Extra food items

In Advance:
- Photocopy and cut out Bible Verse Cards—one per child (page 68). Place in a bin for each Small Group Leader.
- Purchase canned goods or other non-perishable food items. This week, Small Group Leaders will be collecting food items from their Small Groups. Have enough extra food on hand for visitors, new children, or kids who forgot to bring something. Plan for kids to pick the food up at registration, or as they enter the classroom.
- Decide with Small Group Leaders where to donate the food. Oversee the delivery of the food to that location.

Lesson 13

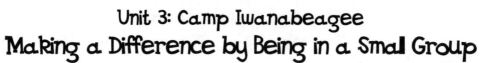

Unit 3: Camp Iwanabeagee
Making a Difference by Being in a Small Group

Activity Stations:
- Choose activities that will work best for this lesson.
- Assist with setup.
- Confirm any guests you have scheduled.
- Offer your support in any way needed.

Large Group Supplies:
- ○ Group Flag
- ○ Campfire (rocks and logs)
- ○ *Camp Iwanabeagee* CD
- ○ Bible Verse sign
- ○ Flip chart/marker
- ○ Music for transitions and singing
- ○ *Optional: Doing Life with God in the Picture CD*

Costumes:
- ○ Camp Counselor clothes

Equipment Needs:
- ○ CD player

In Advance *(Work with the Large Group Producer to administrate the following)*:
- Determine which songs you will use and be prepared to lead or teach them.

- Prepare the Group Flag by writing or painting GROUP on a bandana-sized square of brightly-colored fabric. You will need to post your flag in your teaching area. You can string it onto a flagpole, hang it from the ceiling, or post it on a bulletin board.
- Listen to the *Camp Iwanabeagee* CD tracks 4 and 10 so you know the Marching Chant and the Group G Cheer.
- Have the teacher wear camp counselor gear, such as a hat, khaki shorts, hiking boots, and a t-shirt. You might carry a canteen, whistle, or other camp gear.
- Recruit a CD Player Assistant.
- Rehearse the teaching time.
- Prepare Bible Verse sign.
- Gather props and set teaching area. Set up flip chart. Create a campfire by piling a few logs on your area. Encircle the logs with rocks. If possible, put an orange light inside the logs, and turn it on at campfire time. You can use blinking and non-blinking

orange hazard lights, or Christmas tree lights. You may want to create a camp-like setting on your teaching area, painting a backdrop of a camp cabin, and setting fake Christmas trees, plants, and trees around the teaching area.

Small Group Supplies:
- ○ Bandanas
- ○ Permanent Markers

In Advance:
- Photocopy and cut out Bible Verse Cards—one per child (page 69).
- Gather bandanas—one per child. You can purchase these at craft or variety stores.
- Gather permanent markers—several per Small Group.
- Place the above-mentioned items in a bin for each Small Group Leader.
- Gather games and activities to have on hand for substitute leaders who may not have an activity planned, or for leaders who lead groups of visitors.

Lesson 1
Bases

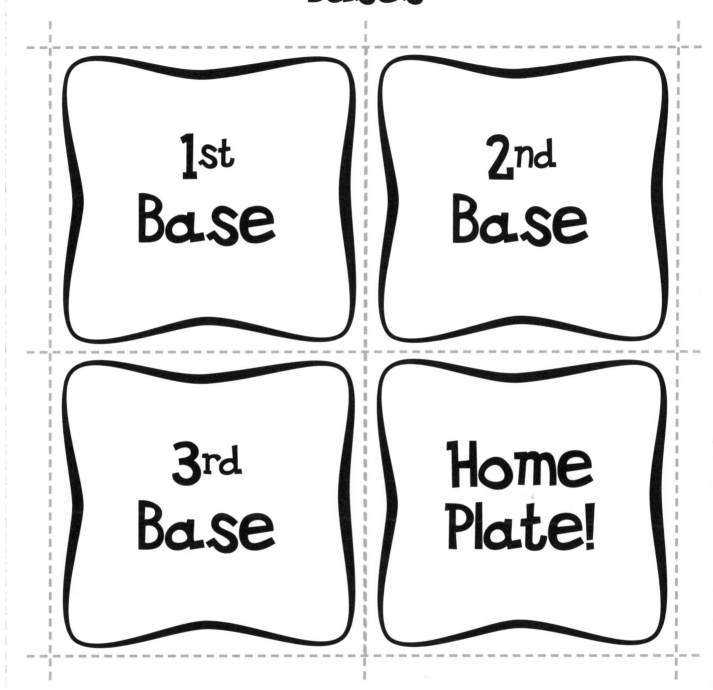

1st Base

2nd Base

3rd Base

Home Plate!

Lesson 1
Game Cards

Pop fly to
right field.
You're OUT!

Pop fly to
right field.
You're OUT!

Pop fly to
left field.
You're OUT!

Pop fly to
left field.
You're OUT!

Pop fly to
center field.
You're OUT!

Pop fly to
center field.
You're OUT!

Shortstop throws
you out at first.
You're OUT!

Shortstop throws
you out at first.
You're OUT!

Lesson 1
Game Cards

How can you be others-centered at home?

(Number of answers=number of bases. The other team judges your answers.)

How can you be others-centered at school?

(Number of answers=number of bases. The other team judges your answers.)

How can you be others-centered at school?

(Number of answers=number of bases. The other team judges your answers.)

How can you be others-centered with your brothers and sisters?

(Number of answers=number of bases. The other team judges your answers.)

How can you be others-centered at the park?

(Number of answers=number of bases. The other team judges your answers.)

How can you be others-centered when you are playing with your friends?

(Number of answers=number of bases. The other team judges your answers.)

How can you be others-centered in your activities, such as sports, art, or music?

(Number of answers=number of bases. The other team judges your answers.)

How can you be others-centered in your activities, such as sports, art, or music?

(Number of answers=number of bases. The other team judges your answers.)

23

Lesson 1
Game Cards

How can you be others-centered at church?

(Number of answers=number of bases. The other team judges your answers.)

How can you be others-centered at church?

(Number of answers=number of bases. The other team judges your answers.)

There is only one piece of cake left and you know your brother loves that cake. What is your first reaction? What could you remember in this situation?

(You hit a Double)

Your mom lets you and your brothers and sisters choose where to go for dinner. Your idea isn't chosen. What is your first reaction? What do you pray for?

(You hit a Single)

Your mom asks you and your sister how your day went. You know your sister had a really bad day, but you answer first and tell your mom all about your great day. Is that being others-centered? Why or why not?

(You hit a Single)

You run to get the best seat in the car. You know your sister gets car sick if she sits the back. What could you do or say that shows an others-centered response?

(You hit a Single)

Your friends play a game you don't like. What is your first reaction? What might help you be more others-centered?

(You hit a Double)

Tell us about a person you know who is others-centered. What does that person do and say that shows you he/she is others-centered?

(You hit a Single)

Lesson 1
Game Cards

Third baseman throws you out at first. You're OUT!

Third baseman throws you out at first. You're OUT!

Pitcher throws you out at first. You're OUT!

Pitcher throws you out at first. You're OUT!

Tell us about a time when someone put you first.

(You hit a Double)

Tell us about a time when you were others-centered.

(You hit a Triple)

Tell us what you can do to train yourself to be others-centered.

(You hit a Double)

You get a new video game at your birthday party. Some of your friends want to try it. What is your first reaction? What do you think Jesus would do in that situation?

(You hit a Triple)

Lesson 1
Score Cards

TEAM A
Runs Scored

TEAM B
Runs Scored

TEAM A
Runs Scored

TEAM B
Runs Scored

5-G Challenge / Spring Quarter / Lesson 1 / Small Group / Score Cards

Lesson 1
Bible Verse Cards

"Each of you should look not only to your own interests, but also to the interests of others."

Philippians 2:4

"Each of you should look not only to your own interests, but also to the interests of others."

Philippians 2:4

"Each of you should look not only to your own interests, but also to the interests of others."

Philippians 2:4

"Each of you should look not only to your own interests, but also to the interests of others."

Philippians 2:4

"Each of you should look not only to your own interests, but also to the interests of others."

Philippians 2:4

"Each of you should look not only to your own interests, but also to the interests of others."

Philippians 2:4

"Each of you should look not only to your own interests, but also to the interests of others."

Philippians 2:4

"Each of you should look not only to your own interests, but also to the interests of others."

Philippians 2:4

"Each of you should look not only to your own interests, but also to the interests of others."

Philippians 2:4

"Each of you should look not only to your own interests, but also to the interests of others."

Philippians 2:4

Lesson 2
Game Cards

You want to call your best friend to tell him/her about the new, very expensive video game you just got. You know your friend has wanted this game forever. How can you tell him/her in a humble way?

You just got your math scores back from the math test. You did much better than your friend. He asks you about your score. What is the humble response?

You just got a perfect score on your spelling test. Your friend is really upset, because she didn't do very well. How could you be humble in this situation?

Have you ever bragged about something? How did it feel?

You think you are better than another person because you have cooler and newer toys than him/her. Is that pride? Why or why not?

How can you train yourself to be humble?

Your team beat your best friend's team 10-1 in baseball. What is the humble thing to say? What is the prideful thing to say?

You scored the winning run during a kick ball game. What is the prideful thing to do? What is the humble thing to do?

You and another person won a math game at school, and you get to choose a sticker from your teacher. There is only one really cool sticker left. What is the humble thing to do? Would being humble be hard or easy?

What does it mean to be prideful?

28

Lesson 2
Game Cards

What does it
mean to be humble?

What is the easiest thing
for you to brag about? Why?

How do you feel when you are
around someone who brags a lot?

What do kids at
school brag about?

You play your piece perfectly at
your piano recital, but your friend
gets nervous and makes lots of
mistakes. How can you have a
humble attitude in this situation?

You are playing a game
with your friends. You all really
want to win. How can you be
humble in that situation?

FUMBLE!
Spell the word, "Mississippi."

FUMBLE!
What does STOP stand for?

FUMBLE!
Say the names of
each person on your team.

FUMBLE!
Name three
professional football teams.

END ZONE TOUCHDOWN

9   8   7   6   5

1   2   3   4   5

5   4   3   2   1

END ZONE TOUCHDOWN

5   6   7   8   9

31

Lesson 2
Score Cards

TEAM A
Points Scored

TEAM B
Points Scored

TEAM A
Points Scored

TEAM B
Points Scored

Lesson 2
Bible Verse Cards

"All who make themselves great will be made humble, but those who make themselves humble will be made great."

Luke 14:11 (NCV)

"All who make themselves great will be made humble, but those who make themselves humble will be made great."

Luke 14:11 (NCV)

"All who make themselves great will be made humble, but those who make themselves humble will be made great."

Luke 14:11 (NCV)

"All who make themselves great will be made humble, but those who make themselves humble will be made great."

Luke 14:11 (NCV)

"All who make themselves great will be made humble, but those who make themselves humble will be made great."

Luke 14:11 (NCV)

"All who make themselves great will be made humble, but those who make themselves humble will be made great."

Luke 14:11 (NCV)

"All who make themselves great will be made humble, but those who make themselves humble will be made great."

Luke 14:11 (NCV)

"All who make themselves great will be made humble, but those who make themselves humble will be made great."

Luke 14:11 (NCV)

"All who make themselves great will be made humble, but those who make themselves humble will be made great."

Luke 14:11 (NCV)

"All who make themselves great will be made humble, but those who make themselves humble will be made great."

Luke 14:11 (NCV)

Lesson 3
Game Cards

Your family is collecting money to buy food for people who don't have much money. How could you make money to give to the collection?

You saved $10 to buy a new video game. Your friend's house just burned down, and he lost all his toys. Do you think you could give him a gift or some of the money? Why or why not?

You received two of the same toys for your birthday. What is your first reaction? What do you think Jesus would do?

You go through some of your toys and see that you don't play with a lot of them. What could you do with them?

Your friend forgot to bring her lunch to school. What could you do to show generosity?

Your friend needs help with her math homework, and you finished yours hours ago. She asks if you can come over and help her, but your favorite TV show is on. What is your first reaction? What do you think Jesus would do?

What things are kids most greedy with at school?

Why do you think people are greedy?

34

Lesson 3
Game Cards

What is one way you
can be generous at home?

Do you know anyone
who is a generous person?
Do you like being around him or her?
Why or why not?

Do you think greedy
people are fun to be around?
Why or why not?

What is one way you can
be generous at school?

What is one thing with
which you are most greedy?

How can you train
yourself to be generous?

There are three pieces of
cake left and four people in
your family. What is the generous
response? Would it be hard to be
generous? Why or why not?

The elderly lady who lives next door
to you just fell and broke her hip.
What are a few things you could
do to be generous to her?

Lesson 3
Score Cards

TEAM A
Goals Scored

TEAM B
Goals Scored

TEAM A
Goals Scored

TEAM B
Goals Scored

Lesson 3
Bible Verse Cards

"Do good...be generous
and willing to share."

I Timothy 6:18

"Do good...be generous
and willing to share."

I Timothy 6:18

"Do good...be generous
and willing to share."

I Timothy 6:18

"Do good...be generous
and willing to share."

I Timothy 6:18

"Do good...be generous
and willing to share."

I Timothy 6:18

"Do good...be generous
and willing to share."

I Timothy 6:18

"Do good...be generous
and willing to share."

I Timothy 6:18

"Do good...be generous
and willing to share."

I Timothy 6:18

"Do good...be generous
and willing to share."

I Timothy 6:18

"Do good...be generous
and willing to share."

I Timothy 6:18

5-G Challenge / Spring Quarter / Lesson 3 / Small Group / Bible Verse Cards

Lesson 4
Game Cards

Who was envious
in today's Bible Story?

(The workers who started work early.)

Why were the workers
envious in today's Bible story?

(Workers who started later than
they did got the same payment.)

What did the landowner say when he
heard the workers were jealous?

(He told them he could be generous
to whomever he wanted, and to
be content with what they had.)

Who told this
story in the Bible?

(Jesus)

What is one way you are
sometimes envious of
someone in your family?

What is one way you are
sometimes envious of a friend?

In Large Group, we learned about a
sentence can you say in order to
stop being envious. What was it?

(I am content with what I have.)

Your friends are talking about the big
test. You got a B, but your friend got a
perfect score, so you start to feel
envious. What can you remember
to help you not be envious?

(the word STOP or the sentence,
"I am content with what I have.")

38

© 2001 Willow Creek Community Church
Permission granted to reproduce this page for use in this program.

5-G Challenge / Spring Quarter / Lesson 4 / Small Group / Game Cards—page 1 of 3

Lesson 4
Game Cards

What kinds of
things make you feel
envious of other people?

Is it hard to be happy
for other people when
they have nice things?
Why or why not?

How can you cross train
yourself to be content?

(The word STOP.)

Your friend got the new video
game you want. Walk through the
word STOP to figure out what to
do in this situation. S? T? O? P?

(Stop. Think that Jesus would be kind.
Obey the Bible—it says not to envy.
Pray for Jesus' help.)

What is the
definition of "content"?

(Being happy with what you have.)

What is the
definition of "envy"?

(Wanting other people's stuff.)

Do you think you are really
content with what you have?

You are envious of someone else
because he/she is a better soccer
player than you. What do you think
Jesus would do in this situation?

Lesson 4
Game Cards

Your friend says he/she gets to stay up until 10:00. You have to go to bed at 8:30. When your friend asks you what time you have to go to bed, you are tempted to lie and say 10:00. Why do you think you are tempted to lie?

(You might be envious.)

Your friend is moving into a new house with a pool with a slide. You are envious, so you think through STOP. You get to O, Obey the Bible. What does the Bible say about envy?

(Do not envy; be content with what you have.)

Do you know anyone you would describe as content? What kind of things does that person do or say?

Your sister got to go to the pool with her friend, and you feel envious. How do you want to treat your sister? What could you say instead?

Do you think that it is hard to stop the sin of envy? Why or why not?

Your friend scored the winning run in kickball and everyone is cheering for him/her. You feel a little envious. What could you pray for?

Name one thing you learned today during Large Group.

What is one situation in which you feel completely content?

Lesson 4
Score Cards

TEAM A
Points Scored

TEAM B
Points Scored

TEAM A
Points Scored

TEAM B
Points Scored

5-G Challenge / Spring Quarter / Lesson 4 / Small Group / Score Cards

Lesson 4
Bible Verse Cards

 "Be content with what you have."
Hebrews 13:5

 "Be content with what you have."
Hebrews 13:5

 "Be content with what you have."
Hebrews 13:5

 "Be content with what you have."
Hebrews 13:5

 "Be content with what you have."
Hebrews 13:5

 "Be content with what you have."
Hebrews 13:5

 "Be content with what you have."
Hebrews 13:5

 "Be content with what you have."
Hebrews 13:5

 "Be content with what you have."
Hebrews 13:5

 "Be content with what you have."
Hebrews 13:5

Lesson 5
Easter Story Pictures

43

Lesson 5
Easter Story Pictures

NO WAY!

Lesson 5
Bible Verse Cards

 "For Christ died for sins once for all...to bring you to God."

I Peter 3:18

 "For Christ died for sins once for all...to bring you to God."

I Peter 3:18

 "For Christ died for sins once for all...to bring you to God."

I Peter 3:18

 "For Christ died for sins once for all...to bring you to God."

I Peter 3:18

 "For Christ died for sins once for all...to bring you to God."

I Peter 3:18

 "For Christ died for sins once for all...to bring you to God."

I Peter 3:18

 "For Christ died for sins once for all...to bring you to God."

I Peter 3:18

 "For Christ died for sins once for all...to bring you to God."

I Peter 3:18

 "For Christ died for sins once for all...to bring you to God."

I Peter 3:18

 "For Christ died for sins once for all...to bring you to God."

I Peter 3:18

45

Lesson 6
STOP Medals

You have been awarded the STOP medal

Stop
Think
Obey
Pray

You have been awarded the STOP medal

Stop
Think
Obey
Pray

Lesson 6
STOP Cards

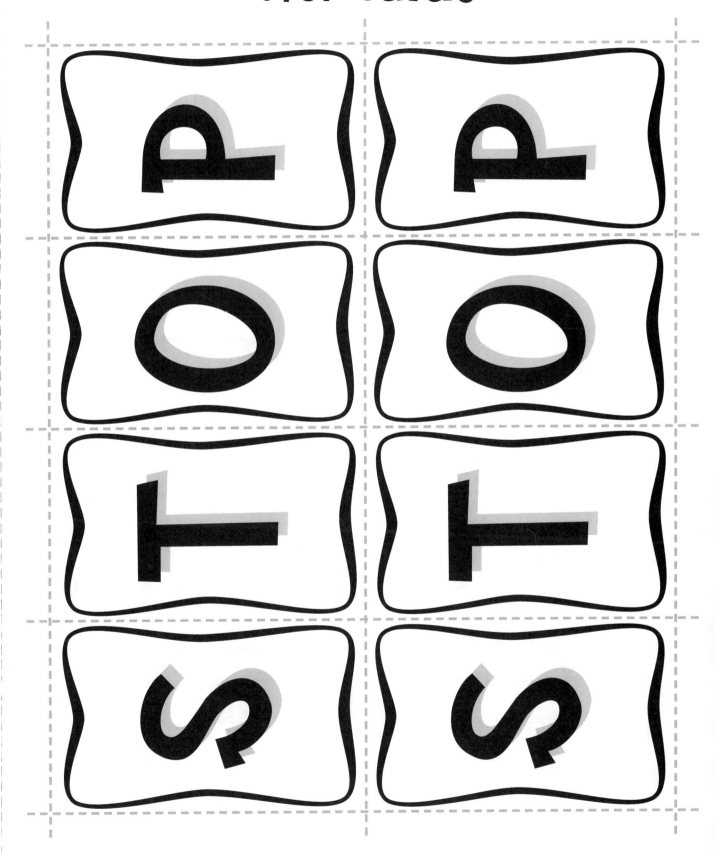

5-G Challenge / Spring Quarter / Lesson 6 / Small Group / STOP Cards

Lesson 6
Bible Verse Cards

 "Forgive as the Lord forgave you."

Colossians 3:13

 "Forgive as the Lord forgave you."

Colossians 3:13

 "Forgive as the Lord forgave you."

Colossians 3:13

 "Forgive as the Lord forgave you."

Colossians 3:13

 "Forgive as the Lord forgave you."

Colossians 3:13

 "Forgive as the Lord forgave you."

Colossians 3:13

 "Forgive as the Lord forgave you."

Colossians 3:13

 "Forgive as the Lord forgave you."

Colossians 3:13

 "Forgive as the Lord forgave you."

Colossians 3:13

 "Forgive as the Lord forgave you."

Colossians 3:13

48

Lesson 7
Mega Memory Cards

Mega Memory!

"Children, obey your parents in the Lord, for this is right."

Ephesians 6:1

Mega Memory!

"So do not fear, for I am with you."

Isaiah 41:10

Mega Memory!

"Love each other as I have loved you."

John 15:12

Mega Memory!

"Forgive as the Lord forgave you."

Colossians 3:13

Lesson 7
Bible Verse Cards

"The Holy Spirit...will remind you of everything I have said to you."

John 14:26

"The Holy Spirit...will remind you of everything I have said to you."

John 14:26

"The Holy Spirit...will remind you of everything I have said to you."

John 14:26

"The Holy Spirit...will remind you of everything I have said to you."

John 14:26

"The Holy Spirit...will remind you of everything I have said to you."

John 14:26

"The Holy Spirit...will remind you of everything I have said to you."

John 14:26

"The Holy Spirit...will remind you of everything I have said to you."

John 14:26

"The Holy Spirit...will remind you of everything I have said to you."

John 14:26

"The Holy Spirit...will remind you of everything I have said to you."

John 14:26

"The Holy Spirit...will remind you of everything I have said to you."

John 14:26

Lesson 8
Power Cards

When you are in a difficult situation, what are the three things you need to do with the Holy Spirit's help?

(Remember, Ask, Do)

In Large Group today, we saw a situation where a girl named Maria felt jealous. What did she remember that helped her realize she shouldn't be jealous?

(A Bible Verse)

In Large Group today, we saw a situation where a girl named Kim felt impatient at the vending machine. What did she pray?

(She prayed for God to help her be patient.)

In Large Group today, we saw a situation where a boy named Brian was disobeying by watching TV. What did he hear that helped him do the right thing?

(A song about God)

What is one thing the Holy Spirit can bring to mind when you are in a difficult situation?

(Bible verse, song about God, something you learned in church)

At school, you saw someone steal something out of another person's desk. You are not sure what to do. What could you do to help you figure out this situation?

(Pray)

Your friend Joe got the new scooter you really want. He came over to your house just to show it to you. You are so jealous! What lesson have you learned in church that can help you?

Think of one song you know about God. Say or sing the chorus for us. What is it telling us about us, or about God?

Lesson 8
Power Cards

What does this Bible Verse tell us about God? "I can do everything through Him who gives me strength." Philippians 4:13

(God will give us strength to face difficult situations.)

"I can do everything through Him who gives me strength." Philippians 4:13. Give an example of a situation where this verse would help you.

You are sleeping over at your friend's house, and you wake up in the middle of the night with a bad dream. What could you do to get the help of the Holy Spirit?

(Remember a Bible verse or song, pray for help.)

Your mom asks you if you finished your homework. You want to lie and say you are finished so you can watch TV. What do you know about God that might help you do the right thing?

(God does not want us to lie; the Bible says not to lie.)

Tell us about a time when you needed to make a decision, and you didn't know what to do. Could you have prayed about that decision? Could the Holy Spirit have helped you in that situation?

Your younger brother colored on your favorite shirt and ruined it. You are very angry. What Bible verse, Bible lesson, or song could help you forgive in this situation?

Your friend wants to cheat off your math paper. What do you REMEMBER about God and the Bible? What do you ASK God to help you with? What do you DO?

How does the Holy Spirit help you?

(Gives you courage, is always with you, and helps you remember what the Bible says.)

52

Lesson 8
Bible Verse Cards

"I can do everything through Him who gives me strength."

Philippians 4:13

"I can do everything through Him who gives me strength."

Philippians 4:13

"I can do everything through Him who gives me strength."

Philippians 4:13

"I can do everything through Him who gives me strength."

Philippians 4:13

"I can do everything through Him who gives me strength."

Philippians 4:13

"I can do everything through Him who gives me strength."

Philippians 4:13

"I can do everything through Him who gives me strength."

Philippians 4:13

"I can do everything through Him who gives me strength."

Philippians 4:13

"I can do everything through Him who gives me strength."

Philippians 4:13

"I can do everything through Him who gives me strength."

Philippians 4:13

5-G Challenge / Spring Quarter / Lesson 8 / Small Group / Bible Verse Cards

Don't miss the fun!

Don't miss the fun!

(Fold 2)

_____ (church name)

_____ (church address)

_____ (church phone number)

_____ (church website)

_____ (service times)

(Fold 1)

Don't miss the fun!

Using the code below, decode the secret message!

A=1	H=8	O=15	V=22
B=2	I=9	P=16	W=23
C=3	J=10	Q=17	X=24
D=4	K=11	R=18	Y=25
E=5	L=12	S=19	Z=26
F=6	M=13	T=20	
G=7	N=14	U=21	

54

Lesson 9
Code Instruction Card

How to write the code:

Write the correct number of spaces for your message. Then, write the correct number under a space to create your code. Your friend will fill in the correct letters. Leave space for your friend to write!

A=1	E=5	I=9	M=13	Q=17	U=21	Y=25
B=2	F=6	J=10	N=14	R=18	V=22	Z=26
C=3	G=7	K=11	O=15	S=19	W=23	
D=4	H=8	L=12	P=16	T=20	X=24	

C O M E   T O
3 15 13 5   20 15

C H U R C H
3 8 21 18 3 8

W I T H   M E
23 9 20 8   13 5

Lesson 9
Bible Verse Cards

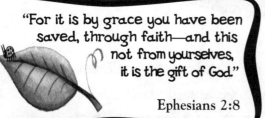

"For it is by grace you have been saved, through faith—and this not from yourselves, it is the gift of God."

Ephesians 2:8

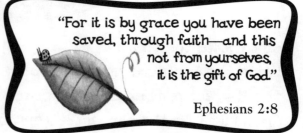

"For it is by grace you have been saved, through faith—and this not from yourselves, it is the gift of God."

Ephesians 2:8

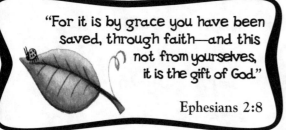

"For it is by grace you have been saved, through faith—and this not from yourselves, it is the gift of God."

Ephesians 2:8

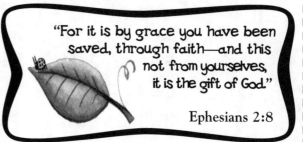

"For it is by grace you have been saved, through faith—and this not from yourselves, it is the gift of God."

Ephesians 2:8

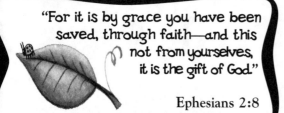

"For it is by grace you have been saved, through faith—and this not from yourselves, it is the gift of God."

Ephesians 2:8

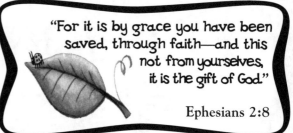

"For it is by grace you have been saved, through faith—and this not from yourselves, it is the gift of God."

Ephesians 2:8

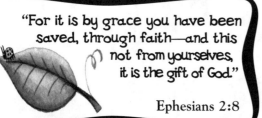

"For it is by grace you have been saved, through faith—and this not from yourselves, it is the gift of God."

Ephesians 2:8

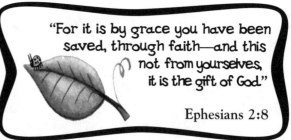

"For it is by grace you have been saved, through faith—and this not from yourselves, it is the gift of God."

Ephesians 2:8

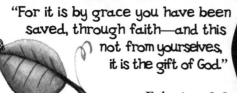

"For it is by grace you have been saved, through faith—and this not from yourselves, it is the gift of God."

Ephesians 2:8

"For it is by grace you have been saved, through faith—and this not from yourselves, it is the gift of God."

Ephesians 2:8

Fruit Cards

You are at your friend's soccer game. He/she scored a goal. What Fruit of the Spirit could you show in this situation? How would you show it?

You are helping your little brother with his math homework. He has to write numbers and he keeps getting them wrong. You are getting frustrated. What Fruit of the Spirit could you show in this situation?

The other kids in your class are teasing your friend because he/she does not play kick ball very well. What Fruit of the Spirit could you show in this situation? What difference would it make to your friend?

You are anxious about a test you have at school. What Fruit of the Spirit could you show?

Whenever your friend comes over to your house, he/she plays with the same toy. One day, you give it to your friend to keep. He/she is so surprised and happy. What Fruit of the Spirit are you showing?

Your friend needs some help with his/her math homework. You say you will help her during the first part of recess. She is still having trouble and recess is almost over. What Fruit of the Spirit could you show? What difference would it make to your friend?

What is one way you could show love to someone in your family? Do you think it would make a difference in your family?

You invite to your house a kid no one likes. What Fruit of the Spirit are you showing? What difference would it make in his/her life?

Lesson 10
Fruit Cards

You and your friend are going away to camp for the first time. You are both a little nervous. What Fruit of the Spirit could you show?

Your mom says you can't go to play at a friend's house. What Fruit of the Spirit could you show? What difference would it make to your mom?

Your mom needs help carrying things to the car, but you really want to race your sister to sit in the best seat. What Fruit of the Spirit would you be showing if you waited to help your mom?

How could you show kindness to someone at school?

What is one way you could show patience to a sister or brother?

How could you show joy at home after school?

How could you show love to one of your grandparents?

How could you show that you have peace in a difficult situation?

Lesson 10
"Know Your Fruit" Square

Lesson 10
Bible Verse Cards

"But the fruit of the Spirit is love, joy, peace, patience, kindness, goodness, faithfulness, gentleness, and self-control."

Galatians 5:22-23

"But the fruit of the Spirit is love, joy, peace, patience, kindness, goodness, faithfulness, gentleness, and self-control."

Galatians 5:22-23

"But the fruit of the Spirit is love, joy, peace, patience, kindness, goodness, faithfulness, gentleness, and self-control."

Galatians 5:22-23

"But the fruit of the Spirit is love, joy, peace, patience, kindness, goodness, faithfulness, gentleness, and self-control."

Galatians 5:22-23

"But the fruit of the Spirit is love, joy, peace, patience, kindness, goodness, faithfulness, gentleness, and self-control."

Galatians 5:22-23

"But the fruit of the Spirit is love, joy, peace, patience, kindness, goodness, faithfulness, gentleness, and self-control."

Galatians 5:22-23

"But the fruit of the Spirit is love, joy, peace, patience, kindness, goodness, faithfulness, gentleness, and self-control."

Galatians 5:22-23

"But the fruit of the Spirit is love, joy, peace, patience, kindness, goodness, faithfulness, gentleness, and self-control."

Galatians 5:22-23

"But the fruit of the Spirit is love, joy, peace, patience, kindness, goodness, faithfulness, gentleness, and self-control."

Galatians 5:22-23

"But the fruit of the Spirit is love, joy, peace, patience, kindness, goodness, faithfulness, gentleness, and self-control."

Galatians 5:22-23

Lesson 10
Parent Letter Example

Dear Parents of Second & Third Graders:

This month in (*name of children's ministry*), your children are a part of a unit called, "Camp Iwanabeagee," where they are learning how they can make a difference in the lives of others. They are experiencing the 5-Gs—Grace, Growth, Good Stewardship, Gifts, and Group—and learning that as they develop each of these Gs in their lives, they can make a difference in the lives of others.

In two weeks, your children will learn about Good Stewardship—giving of our time, resources, and talents. During that lesson, kids will have the opportunity to participate in a giving project. Please have your child bring canned goods and other non-perishable food items to give to a food pantry.

We are encouraging the children to use their own money to purchase one or more items to help make a difference in the lives of other children. In this way, they will learn that they truly can make a difference when they give of their time, resources, or talents.

Please bring the items with you on (*date*). Thank you for supporting this project. If you have any questions, please call (*name*) at (*phone*).

Sincerely,

(*Children's Ministry Director*)

Lesson 11

Self-Control Station Instruction Sheet
Bucket Relay

Materials needed:
- ○ 2 1-gallon buckets with 6 holes punched in the bottom
- ○ 2 large aluminum roasting pans
- ○ 2 1-gallon buckets filled with water
- ○ 6 cups
- ○ Tarp material to place on the floor to protect the carpet

Set-up:
Split your Small Group into two teams. Have each team stand by a roasting pan and place a bucket with holes in each roasting pan. Have two kids stationed to plug the holes in the bucket with their fingers. Place the buckets filled with water at the other end of the game area. The object of the game is to fill the bucket with holes.

To Play:
When you say, "go!" one child from each team must pick up a cup, walk from their bucket with holes to the bucket filled with water, fill up the cup, walk back, and dump the water into the bucket with holes. The child then tags the next person in line to walk down and get more water. The rest of the team needs to take turns plugging the holes in the bucket with their fingers. Be sure to emphasize that to complete this relay, they must use self-control. It will take self-control to plug up the holes and it will take self-control to walk with the cup of water without running or spilling. The first team to fill their bucket wins.

Follow Up Questions:
1 When do you find it hard to show self-control?
2 How do you think you can develop self-control in your life?

Lesson 11

Goodness Station Instruction Sheet
Art

Materials needed:
❍ Large pieces of butcher paper (1 piece per Small Group)
❍ Markers

Directions:
Have one child from your Small Group lay down on a piece of butcher paper.
Using a marker, trace around him/her on the butcher paper. Have that child stand
up. As a group, think of ways you can show goodness to others using our various
body parts. Remember, goodness is being like Jesus in our attitudes and actions.
For example, you can use your hands to help mom wash the dishes. You can use
your mouth to compliment or encourage someone. Think of as many ways as
possible for each body part. Have kids take turns writing the various ways on those
particular body parts on the tracing of the person.

Lesson 11

Gentleness Station Instruction Sheet Story

Materials needed:
○ Various pictures
○ Pencils
○ Paper

Directions:
Display all the pictures for your group to see. Using a few of the pictures, make up a story about a superhero named, "Captain Gentle!" Someone is having a bad day, but Captain Gentle saw it, and he turned it around with gentleness. Create your story, then write it down on the paper provided.

Lesson 11

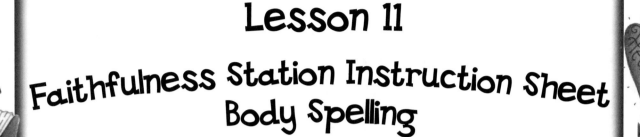

Faithfulness Station Instruction Sheet
Body Spelling

Materials needed:
❍ Pencils
❍ Paper

Directions:
At this station, your Small Group must use their bodies to spell the word FAITH-FUL. You must use everyone in your group to spell every single letter in the word. So, the first letter in Faithful is F. The group must decide how to form an F using everyone on the team. They must continue spelling the rest of the word. When you begin, time your Small Group, and write your time on the paper provided. The group who spells the word in the shortest amount of time wins. (If you have more than ten kids in your group today, split them into two groups to spell the word.)

Follow Up Questions:
1   What is one thing you can do to show faithfulness to God?
2   How can you develop faithfulness to God in your own life?

65

Lesson 11
Bible Verse Cards

"But the fruit of the Spirit is love, joy, peace, patience, kindness, goodness, faithfulness, gentleness, and self-control."

Galatians 5:22-23

"But the fruit of the Spirit is love, joy, peace, patience, kindness, goodness, faithfulness, gentleness, and self-control."

Galatians 5:22-23

"But the fruit of the Spirit is love, joy, peace, patience, kindness, goodness, faithfulness, gentleness, and self-control."

Galatians 5:22-23

"But the fruit of the Spirit is love, joy, peace, patience, kindness, goodness, faithfulness, gentleness, and self-control."

Galatians 5:22-23

"But the fruit of the Spirit is love, joy, peace, patience, kindness, goodness, faithfulness, gentleness, and self-control."

Galatians 5:22-23

"But the fruit of the Spirit is love, joy, peace, patience, kindness, goodness, faithfulness, gentleness, and self-control."

Galatians 5:22-23

"But the fruit of the Spirit is love, joy, peace, patience, kindness, goodness, faithfulness, gentleness, and self-control."

Galatians 5:22-23

"But the fruit of the Spirit is love, joy, peace, patience, kindness, goodness, faithfulness, gentleness, and self-control."

Galatians 5:22-23

"But the fruit of the Spirit is love, joy, peace, patience, kindness, goodness, faithfulness, gentleness, and self-control."

Galatians 5:22-23

"But the fruit of the Spirit is love, joy, peace, patience, kindness, goodness, faithfulness, gentleness, and self-control."

Galatians 5:22-23

Lesson 11
Parent Letter Example

Dear Parents of Second & Third Graders:

This month in (*name of children's ministry*), your children are a part of a unit called, "Camp Iwanabeagee," where they are learning how they can make a difference in the lives of others. They are experiencing the 5-Gs—Grace, Growth, Good Stewardship, Gifts, and Group—and learning that as they develop each of these Gs in their lives, they can make a difference in the lives of others.

Next week, your children will learn about Good Stewardship—giving of our time, resources, and talents. During that lesson, kids will have the opportunity to participate in a giving project. Please have your child bring canned goods and other non-perishable food items to give to a food pantry.

We are encouraging the children to use their own money to purchase one or more items to help make a difference in the lives of other children. In this way, they will learn that they truly can make a difference when they give of their time, resources, or talents.

Please bring the items with you on (*date*). Thank you for supporting this project. If you have any questions, please call (*name*) at (*phone*).

Sincerely,

(*Children's Ministry Director*)

Lesson 12
Bible Verse Cards

"Each one should give as you have decided in your heart to give. You should not be sad when you give, and you should not give because you feel forced to give. God loves the person who gives happily."

II Corinthians 9:7 (NCV)

"Each one should give as you have decided in your heart to give. You should not be sad when you give, and you should not give because you feel forced to give. God loves the person who gives happily."

II Corinthians 9:7 (NCV)

"Each one should give as you have decided in your heart to give. You should not be sad when you give, and you should not give because you feel forced to give. God loves the person who gives happily."

II Corinthians 9:7 (NCV)

"Each one should give as you have decided in your heart to give. You should not be sad when you give, and you should not give because you feel forced to give. God loves the person who gives happily."

II Corinthians 9:7 (NCV)

"Each one should give as you have decided in your heart to give. You should not be sad when you give, and you should not give because you feel forced to give. God loves the person who gives happily."

II Corinthians 9:7 (NCV)

"Each one should give as you have decided in your heart to give. You should not be sad when you give, and you should not give because you feel forced to give. God loves the person who gives happily."

II Corinthians 9:7 (NCV)

"Each one should give as you have decided in your heart to give. You should not be sad when you give, and you should not give because you feel forced to give. God loves the person who gives happily."

II Corinthians 9:7 (NCV)

"Each one should give as you have decided in your heart to give. You should not be sad when you give, and you should not give because you feel forced to give. God loves the person who gives happily."

II Corinthians 9:7 (NCV)

"Each one should give as you have decided in your heart to give. You should not be sad when you give, and you should not give because you feel forced to give. God loves the person who gives happily."

II Corinthians 9:7 (NCV)

"Each one should give as you have decided in your heart to give. You should not be sad when you give, and you should not give because you feel forced to give. God loves the person who gives happily."

II Corinthians 9:7 (NCV)

5-G Challenge / Spring Quarter / Lesson 12 / Small Group / Bible Verse Cards

Lesson 13
Bible Verse Cards

Notes:

_____

_____

_____

_____

_____

_____

_____

_____

_____

_____

_____